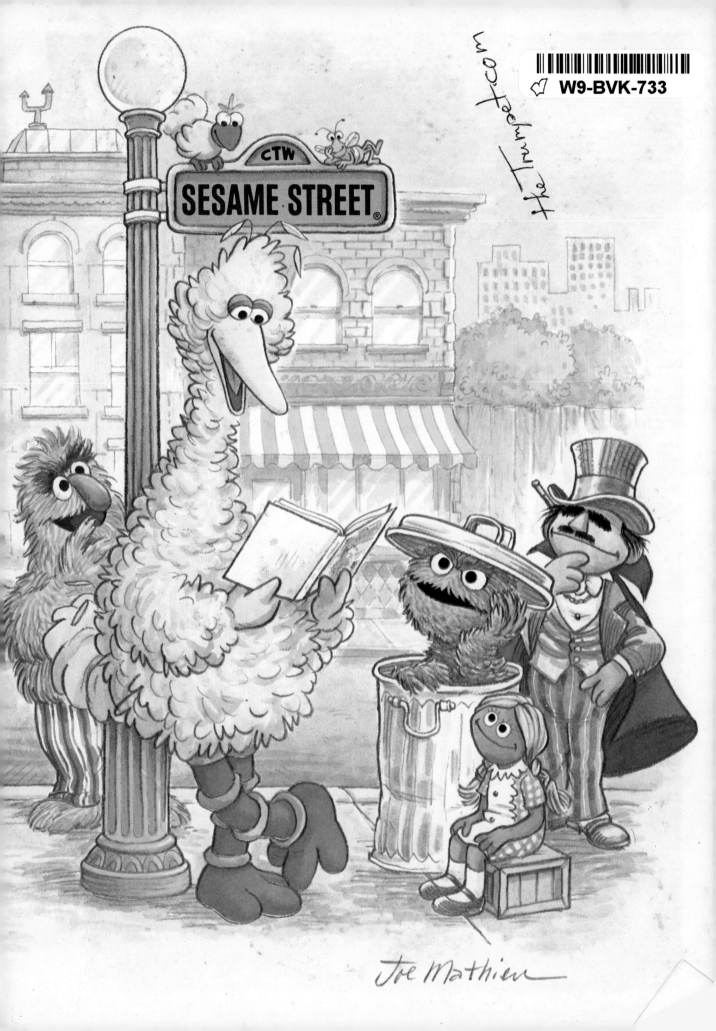

THE SESAME STREET® LIBRARY

With Jim Henson's Muppets

VOLUME 6

FEATURING
THE LETTERS
L AND **M**
AND THE NUMBER
6

Children's Television Workshop/Funk & Wagnalls, Inc.

WRITTEN BY:

Michael Frith
Jerry Juhl
Emily Perl Kingsley
David Korr
Sharon Lerner
Albert G. Miller
Jeffrey Moss
Norman Stiles
Jon Stone
Daniel Wilcox

ILLUSTRATED BY:

Mel Crawford
Michael Frith
Tim and Greg Hildebrandt
Joseph Mathieu
Marc Nadel
Kelly Oechsli

0-8343-0014-1

5 6 7 8 9 0

L 1

The Legend of Lasso Louise

The Lemonade Stand

Oh look!
A lemonade stand.
Everybody bringing
something to help.
Ernie bring sugar.
Count bring 12 lemons
(he counted them).
Bert bring pitcher
of ice water.
Isabella make sign.
That is COOPERATION.
Now guess who help
MIX lemonade…

GULP!

YUM!

OH BOY!

That was very
good lemonade.
And that pitcher
was DELICIOUS!
Sign not bad,
either.
Thanks.

Long, long ago, in a lavish lodge near the village of Liverwurst, lived a lovely lass called Linda the Lonely. Linda was lonely because, ever since she was a little girl, she had been locked in the lodge by her wicked uncle, Lord Ludwig of Liverwurst.

"Alas, alack. What a lousy life I live!" lamented Linda. "Let me loose! Let me loose!"

But Lord Ludwig laughed loudly. "Not likely, my little lamb! I still have loads and loads of work for you to do!"

For long hours Linda labored in Lord Ludwig's library, lifting lots and lots of books. Every day Lord Ludwig would yell, "Linda, you lunk, stop loafing! Where is my lunch? It is late."

Linda lugged Lord Ludwig's large lunch from the larder.

"What have you brought me, you little lump?" asked Lord Ludwig as Linda ladled out his luscious lunch of leafy lettuce, large lobsters, lovely lentils, lima beans, leg of lamb, licorice, lollipops and lemonade.

"Oh, Uncle Ludwig!" Linda lamented, "I have been laboring long hours on your library ladder! Please let me have a little lunch, too."

"Later, lazybones ... if there's any lunch left! Ha, ha! Now leave— and get back to your ladder!"

Late one night, in the loft where she lived, Linda laid her lonely head upon her lumpy little bed. Suddenly she heard voices. Linda leaned out the window to listen.

Lord Ludwig and a lanky lad were on the lawn. "I know I am late with your laundry, Lord Ludwig," said the lad. "But there is so little light and it is such a *large* load of laundry."

"None of your lip, lout! Get a lamp if there is no light—but lather up that laundry or there will be lots of lashes where you least like 'em!"

With that, Lord Ludwig left.

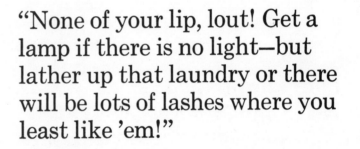

Linda took a lantern and leaned out of the window. She leapt onto the limb of a lemon tree, and lowered herself lightly onto the lawn.

"Who are you?" asked the lanky lad.

"I am Lord Ludwig's niece, Linda the Lonely. Who are you?"

"I am Lloyd of London, Lord Ludwig's lowliest lackey. And I am lonely, too."

"Listen, Lloyd," lilted Linda. "I have long longed to leave this loathsome lodge. Let me tell you my plan! Listen…"

"La," laughed Lloyd. "It's so loony, it just might work!"

Late the next day, Lloyd lugged his load of laundry
into Lord Ludwig's library. "Look, Linda," said Lloyd
as he lifted his lute from under Ludwig's lavender
leggings. "I have brought my lute."

"It's lovely, Lloyd. Now lend me your long leather
laces so I can make a lasso."

Linda told Lloyd
to lull Lord Ludwig
with a lilting
lullaby on his lute.
Soon Lord Ludwig
was fast asleep.

Like lightning, Linda looped her lasso around Lord Ludwig's legs and lashed him to the library ladder.

"Help!" yelled Lord Ludwig. "I want to call my lawyer."

"You'll have lots of time for that, you lily-livered lizard! You're going to learn your lesson. You'll be locked up for a long, long time, laboring in the laundry of the local jail!"

Linda lifted a large key from Ludwig's leather belt, unlocked the lodge's locks and lifted the latch.

"Now, Lloyd, let's leave!" laughed Linda.

"Linda," said Lloyd, "it was a lucky day for me when you leapt from that lemon tree."

"Then we shall call you Lloyd the Lucky," said Linda.

"And you shall be Linda the Lionhearted," said Lloyd.

"And," they said together, "we won't be lonely any longer."

Six Monsters in the Restaurant

The Perils of Penelope

(conclusion)

Fortunately, a Young-Hero-Carpenter happened by in a rowboat, and he added wood to the plank, making it **longer**.

Fear not, Penelope! I, the Young-Hero-Carpenter, happening by in my rowboat, will add wood to the plank, making it longer.

And he made it longer.

And longer…until it led over the roof of Penelope's cottage.

But Penelope spoke too soon. Poor Penelope fell through a weak spot in the roof.

ERNIE'S SIX DELICIOUS COOKIES

When peeking through the oven door,
Old Ernie rubbed his tummy.
He had six cookies baking there,
And, boy, did they look yummy!

When they were done he took them out
And put them on a plate.
But finding them too hot to eat,
He settled down to wait.

The moment Ernie took a chair
To watch the cookies cooling,
The Cookie Monster galloped in,
And, brother, was he drooling!

"Cookie! Cookie! Gimme one!"
The Monster cried. "I eat it!"

"Get going, Monster," Ernie said,
"They're all for me, so beat it!"

"Aw, shucks!" the Cookie Monster growled,
And shuffled out the door.
"He gave up easy," Ernie thought.
"He's not done *that* before."

"And now that I'm alone," he said,
"A cookie I will bite."
But then there entered through the door
A stranger dressed in white.

"Me cookie baker," said the man,
"Me taste your cookies, no?"
"Of course," said Ernie, "help yourself.
Take *two* before you go."

The baker wolfed the cookies down
And hurried out the door.

"He loved my cookies," Ernie said,
"But now I've only four."

The moment he sat down again,
Another stranger came:
A little girl with yellow hair,
Who called out Ernie's name.

"Me hungry, Ernie," growled the girl.
"You cookies got for me?"

"I've only four left," Ernie said,
"But I will give you three."

She swallowed all three cookies whole

And galloped out the door.

And Ernie had one cookie left,
Of all his yummy four.

Then Bert came in and said, "Hey, Ern,
I just saw something wild—
The Cookie Monster just came out,
Dressed like a little child."

"The Cookie Monster?" Ernie cried.
"That really makes me sore!
He ate two cookies first time here,
And then he ate three more!"

Said Bert, "I see you saved *me* one,
I'll eat it now, right here."
And snatching Ernie's cookie up,
He made it disappear.

Poor Ernie eyed the empty plate
And groaned, "What happened, son?
You baked six cookies for yourself,
And ate not even one!"